QED WordBanks

Learning Words with Monsters

MUP'S

Days of the Week

First published in the UK in 2005 by
QED Publishing
A Quarto Group company
226 City Road
London EC1V 2TT
www.qed-publishing.co.uk

A Catalogue record for this book is available from the British Library.

ISBN 1 84538 184 X

Written by Wendy Body
Designed by Alix Wood
Editor Hannah Ray
Illustrated by Sanja Rescek

Series Consultant Anne Faundez
Publisher Steve Evans
Creative Director Louise Morley
Editorial Manager Jean Coppendale

Printed and bound in China

Learning Words with Monsters

MUP'S

Days of the Week

Wendy Body

QED Publishing

On **Monday**, Mup climbed a mountain with a rainbow in his pocket.

Monday

Tuesday

Wednesday

Thursday

Friday

Saturday

Sunday

On **Tuesday**, he flew to the moon and back in a shiny, silver rocket.

6

Monday

Tuesday

Wednesday

Thursday

Friday

Saturday

Sunday

On **Wednesday**, he walked to the North Pole and played with a polar bear.

Monday

Tuesday

Wednesday

Thursday

Friday

Saturday

Sunday

On **Thursday**, he made an enormous cake for all his friends to share.

Monday

Tuesday

Wednesday

Thursday

Friday

Saturday

Sunday

On **Friday**, he had a ride on a whale and went sailing all over the sea.

Monday

Tuesday

Wednesday

Thursday

Friday

Saturday

Sunday

On **Saturday**, he built a castle at the top of a very tall tree.

Monday

Tuesday

Wednesday

Thursday

Friday

Saturday

Sunday

On **Sunday**, he went in a hot-air balloon to fly all over the sky, and painted the clouds with purple paint when they came drifting by.

Monday

Tuesday

Wednesday

Thursday

Friday

Saturday

Sunday

17

Mup's Diary

Monday
climbed a mountain

Tuesday
flew to the moon

Wednesday
walked to the North Pole

Thursday
made an enormous cake

Friday
sailed on a whale

Saturday
built a castle

Sunday
 painted the clouds

Things to do

Can you complete the sentences by pointing to the right day of the week?

Monday
Saturday
Wednesday
Friday
Thursday
Sunday
Tuesday

On _____ Mup climbed a mountain.

On _____ Mup flew to the moon.

On _____ Mup walked to the North Pole.

On _____ Mup made an enormous cake.

On _____ Mup went on a whale.

On _____ Mup built a castle.

On _____ Mup painted the clouds.

Things to do

Can you remember how the words for these pictures begin?

Which words begin with the same sound?

Word bank

Words from the story

balloon
bear
cake
castle
cloud
moon
mountain
pocket
rainbow
rocket
sea
tree
whale

Action words

built
climbed
flew
painted
played
walked

Word bank

Words and endings		**More action words**
build	built	draw
climb	climbed	hop
fly	flew	jump
paint	painted	run
play	played	skip
walk	walked	sit
		swim
What do you notice		stand
about these words?		

23

Parents' and teachers' notes

- As you read the book to your child, run your finger along underneath the text. This will help your child to follow the reading and focus on the look of the words, as well as their sound.
- Once your child is familiar with the book, encourage him or her to join in with the reading – especially the days of the week.
- Help your child to both see and understand the illustrations. Use open-ended questions to encourage him or her to respond, e.g. 'What's happening on this page?' 'What is Mup doing here?' 'Could he really do that?'
- Practise saying the days of the week in order.
- Can your child remember what Mup did on particular days?
- Encourage your child to express opinions and preferences. Ask questions such as, 'Which picture do you like most? Why?' 'Which part of the book did you like best?' 'Which day do you think Mup enjoyed most?' 'If you could do any of the things that Mup did, which would you choose? Why?'
- Ask your child to make comparisons between Mup and himself or herself, e.g. 'Today is Monday (for example). What did Mup do yesterday? What did you do yesterday?' Discuss what your child might do over the course of a week. Are there certain things he or she does on particular days?
- Talk about Mup and discuss the monster's appearance. Encourage your child to invent and describe a monster of his or her own. What things would the monster like to do? What might feature in the monster's diary?

- Draw your child's attention to the structure of some words – especially the days of the week. Look at how each one includes the smaller word 'day'. Explain that this can help us to remember how the words are spelled, e.g. 'Wednesday' is spelled 'Wed–nes–day'.
- Read the instructions/questions on the 'Things to do' pages (pages 20–21) to your child and help him or her with the answers where necessary. Give your child lots of encouragement and praise. Even if he or she gets something wrong you can say: 'That was a really good try but it's not that one it's this one.'
- Read and discuss the words on the 'Word bank' pages (pages 22–23). Look at the letter patterns together and how the words are spelled. Cover up the first part of a word and see if your child can remember what was there. See if your child can write the simpler words from memory – he or she is likely to need several attempts to write a word correctly!
- When you are talking about letter sounds, try not to add too much of an uh or er sound. Say mmm instead of muh or mer, ssss instead of suh or ser. Saying letter sounds as carefully as possible will help your child when he or she is trying to build up or spell words – ter-o-per doesn't sound much like 'top'!
- Talk about words: what they mean, how they sound, how they look and how they are spelled; but if your child gets restless or bored, stop. Enjoyment of the story, activity or book is essential if we want children to grow up valuing books and reading!